This Book Belongs To

Help! The Wolf is Coming!

By Sigal Adler

Many years ago, in a land so far away

Lived a shepherd family who worked hard every day

Among mountains so high, and hillsides so steep

Their three older sons all took care of the sheep.

The three older brothers had flocks of their own,

But the youngest one still had to wait till he'd grown,

He wished to grow big like his brothers, so strong

So he'd have his own sheep before very long.

The brothers would tell him his life was so easy,

Playing in the hills and the valleys, so breezy

They knew he'd be busy soon watching his flock

And then there'd be no time to laugh or to talk.

For there in the mountains so quiet and still

Lurked a grave danger behind every hill.

There the shepherds knew they could never relax,

Lest the enemy strike when they'd turned their backs.

There lurked wolves so hungry, just waiting to strike

If some lazy shepherd took off on a hike.

They hid in the forest, stood behind trees

Sniffing the smell of the sheep on the breeze.

If one saw a wolf he would raise a great shout,

"Help, help! It's a wolf!" he'd scream and cry out;

Then they'd all band together, as quick as you please

To chase those bad wolves back up to the trees.

Well, after some time, the great day came at last,

The boy had grown up and his childhood past;

His father said, "Son, you will be on your own,

"With your very own flock now that you're fully grown."

That night he could barely sleep in his bed

As thoughts of his own sheep raced round his head;

In the morning he left for the fields near their farm

And his brothers said, "If you need us, just call an alarm."

He chose a nice field where the sheep could all graze

And stood there so proudly, a glint in his gaze;

He watched the birds fly past, he watched the bright flowers,

But he began to grow bored after just a few hours.

How long he had dreamed for this day he had planned...

Who knew it would turn out so boring and bland?

He'd hoped for adventure, a challenge, fresh air,

But all the sheep did was just eat grass and stare.

At last, when he could stand there no more

He figured out how to get rid of the bore.

"Help, help! A wolf!" he cried, from the top of a hill.

And his brothers' red faces appeared – what a thrill!

They were panting from running; they were all out of breath,

And their faces were red, like he'd scared them to death.

"Ha, ha!" he laughed loud. "Look at all of you run!"

But the brothers all scolded, "Don't do that for fun!"

But the trick had been so fun he couldn't resist,

And he was so bored there, his staff held in his fist

So at last he knew he would try it again

Climbed up high and shouted, "Help, me!" – so plain.

Again, they all came, panting and red in the face,

"Ha, ha!" the young man laughed. "What a funny race!"

This time they were angrier still, said they'd tell their dad

About his rude game – yes, all three were that mad.

But that night they were tired after how they'd been scared

So the young man went to bed, grateful to be spared.

They didn't tell their father, so he didn't have to pay

For the little game that he'd played on them that day.

A few more days passed, in boredom and peace

Counting the sheep and stroking their soft fleece;

He thought perhaps he'd try his little trick for show –

But then he climbed up the hill – and saw a wolf below!

"Help, help! A wolf!" he cried, terror in his tone,

But no matter how he yelled, he still remained alone.

The brothers heard his cries, you see, but thought it was a game

They feared if they came running it would all turn out the same.

"Help!" he called. "There's a wolf after me!"

But his brothers all figured they knew what they'd see.

The brothers stood and smiled, as their flocks grazed around,

Hoping he would someday learn to grow up and calm down.

"It's not a joke!" the young man cried. "The wolf is really here!"

But all his brothers shook their heads without a trace of fear.

The wolf came close although he tried to chase it far away,

He found himself in battle now – for real, and not for play.

His brothers would not come, he knew, to fight there at his side

So he stood alone and fought, or at least he really tried.

The young man fought like a hero, alone,

Striking the wolf with rocks he had thrown.

After an hour of fighting, the wolf departed

With two of his sheep, he saw broken-hearted.

That young man sure learned his lesson that day

Even if he'd had to learn the hard way;

Never cry for help if that isn't what you need

If you want to be believed, then you must not mislead.

I'm sure the moral of this tale is very, very clear

Don't cry "Wolf!" unless you see a wolf is coming near

The truth is precious, so we must

Never lie to earn our trust.

Adler.sigal@gmail.com

Made in the USA
Lexington, KY
20 August 2018